My Parents are Divorced, My Elbows Have Nicknames, and Other Facts about Me

by Bill Cochran · Illustrated by Steve Björkman

HarperCollinsPublishers

Library of Congress Cataloging-in-Publication Data
Cochran, Bill.
    My parents are divorced, my elbows have nicknames, and other facts about me / by Bill
Cochran ; illustrated by Steve Björkman. — 1st ed.
        p.   cm.
    Summary: While describing his not-so-weird life with his divorced parents, a young boy
also describes some other things about himself that could be considered weird.
    ISBN 978-0-06-053942-9 (trade bdg.) — ISBN 978-0-06-053943-6 (lib bdg.)
    [1. Divorce—Fiction. 2. Parent and child—Fiction. 3. Individuality—Fiction.]
I. Björkman, Steve, ill. II. Title.
PZ7.C63927My 2009   2008005794
[E]—dc22   CIP
                                                                              AC

Typography by Jeanne L. Hogle
1 2 3 4 5 6 7 8 9 10
❖
First Edition

Hi.

My name is Ted and my parents are divorced.
But that doesn't mean I'm weird.

Another thing you should know about me is that I go to sleep every night with just one sock on. Right foot or left foot—it doesn't matter. And that, according to some, may mean I'm a little weird.

But then again,
that's just how I sleep.

When my parents got divorced, my dad moved into his own place on the other side of town. I go there on the weekends, and we listen to some of his old CDs together. I have my own room there, and it's almost as messy as my room at home. I usually come back to my mom's house after dark on Sunday night. It bums me out whenever I have to leave one house to go to the other.

But that doesn't mean I'm weird.

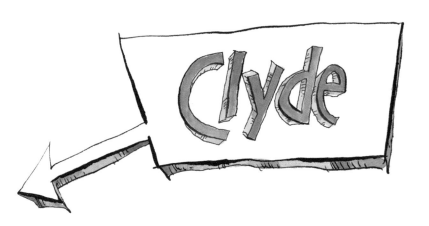

I have nicknames for each of my elbows. My right elbow's name is Carl. My left elbow's name is Clyde. I've pretty much stopped telling people about this. Most of them do, in fact, think it's pretty weird.

Fair enough.

My dad isn't very good at cooking, so after he moved out we had pizza delivered a lot. I love pizza more than anything in the world, but there's just something nice about having homemade food. It took Dad a little while, but now he's learned to make these yummy burritos. We make them together.

Now I think I actually like them even better than delivery pizza.

But that doesn't mean I'm weird.

Sometimes I make soap Mohawks with my hair when I'm in the bathtub. I like to walk around the house with the soap still in my hair. I've done this at my mom's house and my dad's house. Both of them think that it's a little weird.

But I'm just having fun.

A little while after my parents got divorced,
my dad got remarried. So now I have a stepmother.
At first I didn't like her at all, and I'm not even
sure why. It didn't matter how nice she was to me;
I was kind of mean to her.

But now she listens to CDs and makes burritos with us, and the truth is she's not bad. I actually kind of like her.

But that doesn't mean I'm weird.

Sometimes I answer the phone and pretend to be a chicken.
Even I know that's just plain weird.

The fact that I occasionally eat cold spaghetti
sauce by the spoonful straight out of the jar?
Well, I've been told that is, indeed, a bit odd.
Hey, at least I use a spoon.

My parents come to watch my soccer games. Dad stands at one end with my stepmother, and my mom watches at the other. Mom yells a lot louder than Dad. I love seeing them on the sidelines, but it makes me kind of sad that they don't watch together.

My dad's better at helping me with my math homework, but I always seem to have the toughest math homework when I'm with Mom.

My mom's better at putting bandages on me when I skin my knee, and, well, I skin my knees all the time.

A lot of times I miss my mom when I'm at my dad's, and a lot of times I miss my dad when I'm at my mom's.

But that doesn't mean I'm weird.

I wore a cape for Halloween last year, and it made me feel like a superhero. So I wear it a lot, even though it's not Halloween.

And you might think that's weird, but then
again, maybe that's just because you haven't worn
a cape in a while.

The day my parents sat me down to tell me they were getting divorced was probably the worst day of my life. At first it made my stomach feel like I had just stepped off one of those whirly rides at the amusement park, without any of the fun that comes from them.

And then it made me cry—hard. My mom held me for a while, and then my dad held me. I hated it that they couldn't hold me at the same time.

I hated it.

But that doesn't mean I'm weird.

That's just the way it was.

The truth is, I still think about the divorce, and it still hurts every night.

But every day it feels just a little bit better.

Most of all, I've learned that no matter where my mom and dad are, I know they still love me.

Me. A one-sock-sleeping, elbow-nicknaming, soap-Mohawking, chicken-phone-talking, spaghetti-sauce-out-of-the-jar-eating, cape-wearing son of divorced parents.

And maybe that's weird, but . . .

to me, it feels just like me.

And that feels pretty good.